The Bear went over the Mountain

Jane Cabrera

 HOLIDAY HOUSE • NEW YORK

The Bear went over the mountain,
The Bear went over the mountain,
The Bear went over the mountain,
To see what he could see.

But all that he could see.

But all that he could see.

Was the other side of the mountain,

The other side of the mountain,

The other side of the mountain,

Then he got stuck up a tree!

The Hare hopped over the mountain,
The Hare hopped over the mountain,
The Hare hopped over the mountain,
To see where Bear could be.

To see where Bear could be.
To see where Bear could be.

On the other side of the mountain,

The other side of the mountain,

The other side of the mountain,

She helped to set Bear free.

The Fox danced over the mountain,
The Fox danced over the mountain,
The Fox danced over the mountain,
To see where Hare could be.

To see where Hare could be.

To see where Hare could be.

On the other side of the mountain,

The other side of the mountain,

The other side of the mountain,

He made them cups of tea.

The Wolf ran over the mountain,
The Wolf ran over the mountain,
The Wolf ran over the mountain,
To see where Fox could be.

To see where Fox could be.

To see where Fox could be.

On the other side of the mountain,

The other side of the mountain,

The other side of the mountain,

They splashed around with glee!

The Owl swooped over the mountain,
The Owl swooped over the mountain,
The Owl swooped over the mountain,
To see where Wolf could be.

To see where Wolf could be.

To see where Wolf could be.

On the other side of the mountain,
The other side of the mountain,
The other side of the mountain,

They had a Jamboree!
YIPPEE!

I crept over the mountain,

I crept over the mountain,

I crept over the mountain,

To see where they could be.

To see where they could be.

To see where they could be.

On the other side of the mountain,

The other side of the mountain,

The other side of the mountain,

All snuggled up with me.